Willadeen
THE RAINBOW QUEEN

WRITTEN BY CANDACE ROGERS FOX

ILLUSTRATED BY ELIZABETH ROSE HOFFMAN

Author Dedication~
It is true. The greatest gift of all is LOVE. This storybook is inspired
by Willadeen, our adventurous country poodle pup and my beloved
Grandchildren. Being their "Granny" has been one of the greatest joys of my
life. I dedicate this storybook to Ashlyn Jane, Kenna Brooke, Rowen Claire,
Beauden James and for those yet to come. May they remember we can only
live one life, but through the love of reading we can experience many.

Publishing Imprint: CRF Publications. Edited by Carole Baum,
Print Edition: 1st (Nov 2022)
ISBN: 978-1-0880-3845-1

Willadeen
THE RAINBOW QUEEN

WRITTEN BY CANDACE ROGERS FOX
ILLUSTRATED BY ELIZABETH ROSE HOFFMAN

Willadeen is the only poodle pup who lives in the tiny town of Woodburn, Kentucky. Willa, as her family and friends call her, enjoys the country life. She loves sunny days splashing in the creek, running through rainy day puddles, and days when the wind blows through her fluffy fur.

Every morning at sunrise, she prances around as if she is the luckiest pup in the world.

Willadeen spent the first year of her life finding all kinds of adventure. The only thing she loves more than her family is the thrill of a chase. She loves running after butterflies, lightning bugs, and especially rainbows.

Her family has rescued her many times from getting into a whole heap of trouble. Already this summer, she has been sprayed by a skunk, chased by a cow, and pecked on the ear by an angry rooster.

One particularly bright sunny morning, Willadeen's ears perked up at the sound of Granny's voice, "Breakfast is ready!" Doggy slobber hits the floor at the smell of blueberry waffles and bacon. Willadeen watches all the grandchildren sit around the table holding hands, while they listen to Granny once again end her prayer by saying, "May we always remember to walk by faith even when we cannot see."
During breakfast, Granny reminded her three granddaughters and grandson, "Don't forget to put Willa's hiking bell around her neck so y'all can keep track of her on the bike ride today."

As soon as the grandchildren finished their breakfast, they jumped on their bikes and rode off with Willadeen proudly leading the way.

The grandchildren looked like a pack of happy hound dogs chasing a country poodle pup. They all felt in their bones it was going to be a wonderful day!

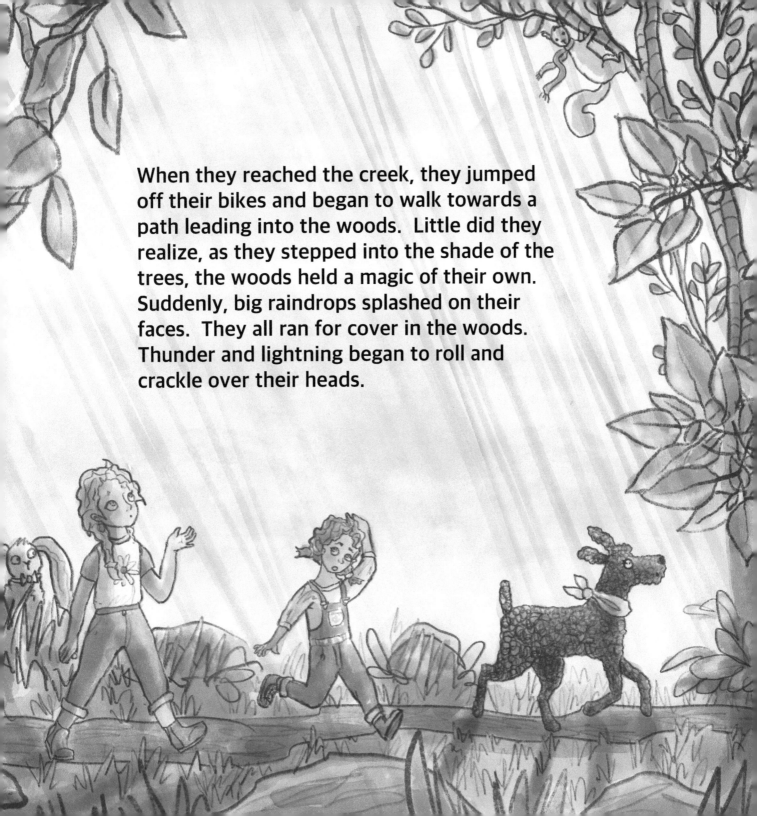

When they reached the creek, they jumped off their bikes and began to walk towards a path leading into the woods. Little did they realize, as they stepped into the shade of the trees, the woods held a magic of their own. Suddenly, big raindrops splashed on their faces. They all ran for cover in the woods. Thunder and lightning began to roll and crackle over their heads.

As they gathered at the edge of the woods, a little white squirrel in a red scarf scurried back and forth in front of a gigantic rock. The squirrel stopped and pointed to a small opening to a hidden cave. "Hey y'all, come over here," she yelled. As each of the children followed the squirrel, they thanked their new friend for saving them from the storm.
"My friends call me Tess," said the squirrel in a squeaky voice. They all sat in the opening of the cave and talked and laughed with Tess, waiting for the storm to pass.

As soon as the rain stopped, Willadeen bolted out of the cave. She barked loudly at something bright and shiny high in the sky. By the time they all came out of the cave, the flash in the sky had disappeared behind the trees. The children watched Willadeen's paws fly off the ground as she quickly ran down the trail and completely out of sight."

The children ran as fast as they could, but they couldn't keep up with Willadeen. Finally, they stopped and looked at each other. The oldest granddaughter cried out, "Oh no, we forgot to put the hiking bell on Willa even after Granny reminded us!" The leaves rustled behind them and all the children turned around in surprise to see Tess, their new squirrel friend, following close behind them. Suddenly a group of bright, yellow butterflies appeared and fluttered ahead down the trail. Everyone chased after them as they hollered and whistled for Willadeen.

Meanwhile, back at the farmhouse, Granny jumped out of her chair when she first heard the cracks of thunder. She peeked out her kitchen window and saw the dark clouds quickly headed their way. She glanced by the door and noticed Willadeen's hiking bell still on its hook. She sighed, "Oh my, they forgot the hiking bell for Willa!" She grabbed her rain hat, coat, and the hiking bell, and jumped into her Jeep to search the countryside for her grandchildren and Willadeen.

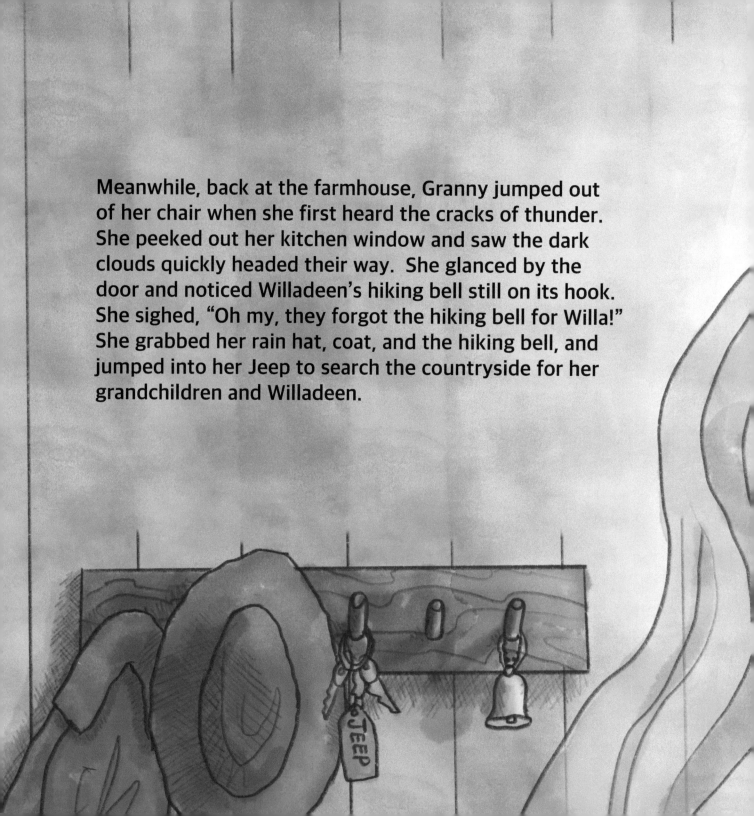

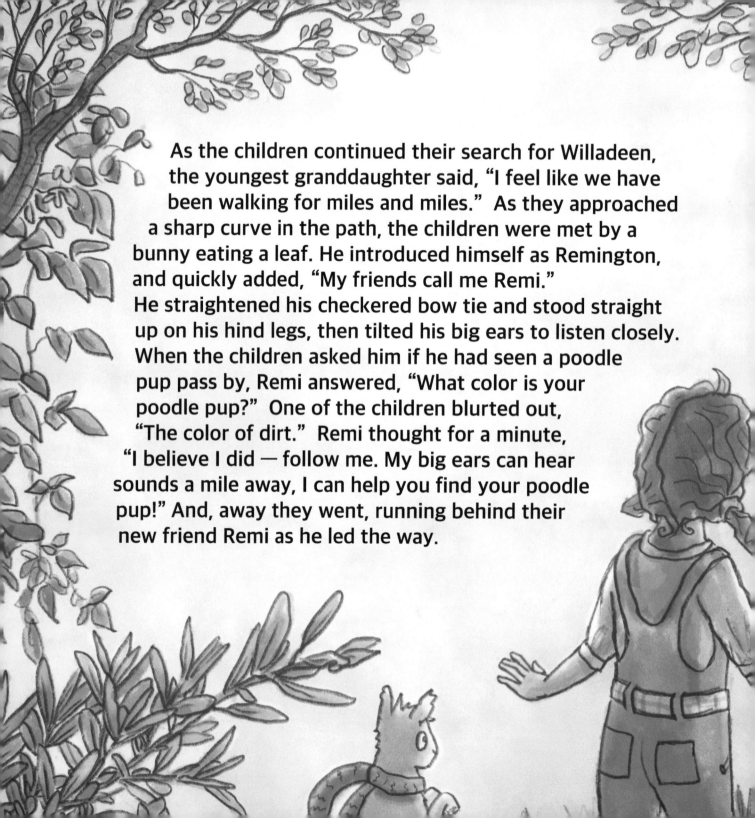

As the children continued their search for Willadeen, the youngest granddaughter said, "I feel like we have been walking for miles and miles." As they approached a sharp curve in the path, the children were met by a bunny eating a leaf. He introduced himself as Remington, and quickly added, "My friends call me Remi." He straightened his checkered bow tie and stood straight up on his hind legs, then tilted his big ears to listen closely. When the children asked him if he had seen a poodle pup pass by, Remi answered, "What color is your poodle pup?" One of the children blurted out, "The color of dirt." Remi thought for a minute, "I believe I did — follow me. My big ears can hear sounds a mile away, I can help you find your poodle pup!" And, away they went, running behind their new friend Remi as he led the way.

Somewhere ahead, Willadeen paused on the trail to shake the mud from her paws. She knew she should wait for her family, but she just couldn't stop running as fast as she could to find that bright flash in the sky. She felt if she were able to catch it her family would be so proud of her that she couldn't possibly get in trouble this time.

Back in the middle of the woods, the three sisters stopped when they heard their little brother screaming behind them. They turned around to look, but he was not there. He must have fallen behind! They all ran back towards the sound of his voice. "Help! Help!" He yelled! They found their brother who had tripped, slipped, and tumbled down a steep hill. The ground was too slippery for him to get back up. All of a sudden . . .

. . . a large gray owl with one pink feather flew out of nowhere. She carried a long vine in her claws. She dropped one end of the vine down to the boy and told him to hold on tightly. Then she flew him up to the open embrace of his sisters. The children thanked the owl and asked what her name was. She replied, "My name is Whisper, but you can call me Wisp." One of the children asked, "Wisp, have you seen a country poodle pup go by?" Wisp opened her eyes wide in surprise. "I sure did, I most certainly did! She was in a big hurry, come on, follow me!" And, away they all went as fast as they could.

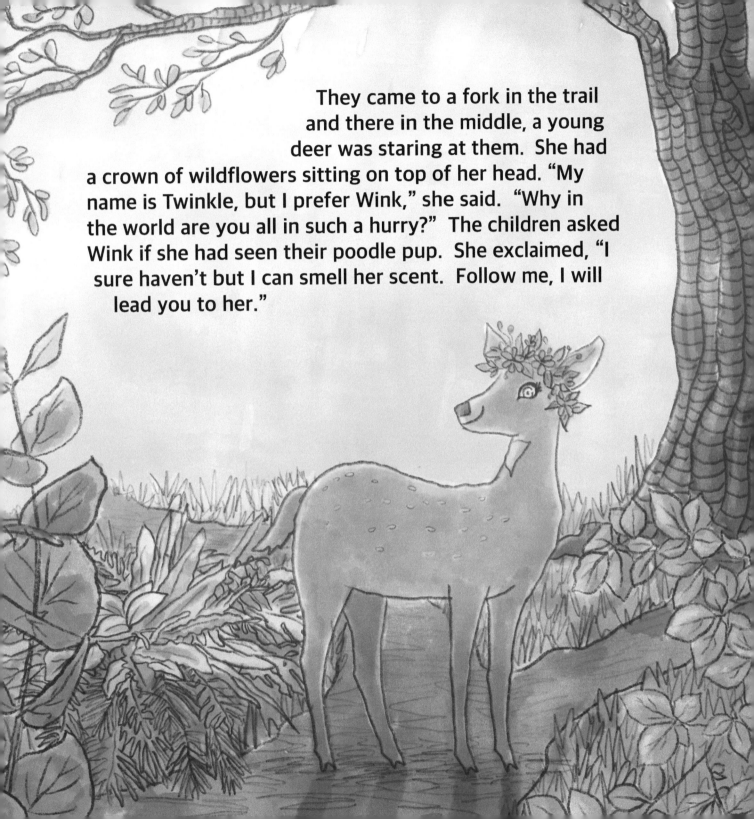

They came to a fork in the trail and there in the middle, a young deer was staring at them. She had a crown of wildflowers sitting on top of her head. "My name is Twinkle, but I prefer Wink," she said. "Why in the world are you all in such a hurry?" The children asked Wink if she had seen their poodle pup. She exclaimed, "I sure haven't but I can smell her scent. Follow me, I will lead you to her."

They ran and ran and ran. Finally, they stopped to catch their breath. They were tired and worried they wouldn't find Willadeen. Just as they were about to give up, they noticed a red fox dressed in a green velvet coat gathering a pile of sticks.

The fox was so startled by the group of children and animals that he dropped his armful of sticks. He straightened his tiny round glasses on the end of his nose and introduced himself. "My name is Sylvester, but most of my friends call me Sly." He asked, "What are you all doing here?" The children asked Sly if he had seen a poodle pup go by. "I sure did," he replied. "Just a few minutes ago. Follow me, I will lead the way!" One after another, they all followed Sly deeper into the woods.

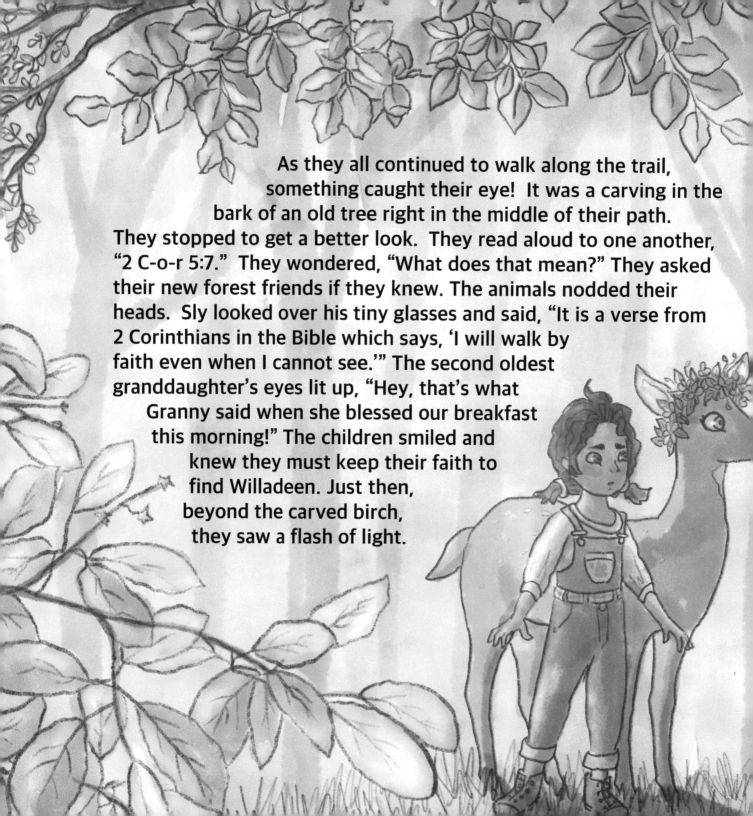

As they all continued to walk along the trail, something caught their eye! It was a carving in the bark of an old tree right in the middle of their path. They stopped to get a better look. They read aloud to one another, "2 C-o-r 5:7." They wondered, "What does that mean?" They asked their new forest friends if they knew. The animals nodded their heads. Sly looked over his tiny glasses and said, "It is a verse from 2 Corinthians in the Bible which says, 'I will walk by faith even when I cannot see.'" The second oldest granddaughter's eyes lit up, "Hey, that's what Granny said when she blessed our breakfast this morning!" The children smiled and knew they must keep their faith to find Willadeen. Just then, beyond the carved birch, they saw a flash of light.

The most amazing rainbow they had ever seen appeared high in the sky through a small opening in the woods in front of them. They all shouted in excitement, "This must be what Willadeen was chasing!" They all knew how much Willadeen loved to chase rainbows.

The grandchildren and their new friends ran as fast as their legs could go. The woods opened up into a big field of wildflowers and there in the middle sat Willadeen on a pile of flat rocks. She was staring up at a big, bright, rainbow that was shining over the pond. When Willadeen heard her family's excited voices, she jumped for joy!

The grandchildren reached Willadeen and gave her a big hug, forming a wall of happiness. They had only seen a rainbow this incredible in storybooks. Willadeen was so thankful her family was not mad at her for running away.

Willadeen's ears
perked up with the familiar
sound of her bell ringing across the
field. They all looked and saw Granny's
silver braids flying as she ran and hollered
to greet them. When she reached them, she
gratefully squeezed them tight, relieved they all
were safe and sound. She was happy they had found
Willadeen and loved meeting their new forest friends.
The children told Granny all about their adventures in the
woods and how each of their new friends had helped them.
They told her about finding the carved Bible verse on a tree,
and how it inspired them to have faith to find Willadeen. Granny
blinked away tears and her voice cracked as she began to speak.

"Long ago, when I was a small girl, I wandered off from home and got lost in these woods. That same tree you found today gave me shade and rest many years ago when I was lost in the woods. I remember feeling so tired and scared. Right before I fell asleep, I prayed someone would find me. When I woke up, my Daddy was standing there. Before he took me back home, he carved that special verse in the tree as a reminder that God does answer prayers. He has answered so many of mine over the years. I prayed that I would find each of you safe today and He has faithfully answered my prayer again." The grandchildren were amazed and thankful that their great-grandfather had found their grandmother that day so long ago.

The oldest granddaughter asked Granny another question. "Is that ole Irish tale really true? Is there really a pot of gold at the end of every rainbow?" Granny smiled and giggled, "Oh, my dear ones. The real pot of gold isn't money or all the things we find ourselves collecting in life; but rather, it is our treasured relationships on earth with the ones we love and the dear friends we meet along the way. That's what life is truly all about! "

They all smiled and nodded their heads.
Then everyone jumped up, joined hands,
and danced joyfully in a circle as the
rainbow slowly began to fade away.

Willadeen jumped high in the air with a nod of her head and a hearty bark. Once again she felt like the luckiest poodle pup in the world. She wagged her tail and ran to give each of the children a big slobbery kiss. They all laughed and declared, "Willa, you will forevermore be known as Woodburn's very own, Willadeen the Rainbow Queen!"

Candace Rogers Fox is a native Kentuckian and Western Kentucky University alum. Candace was born and raised in Danville, Kentucky and has resided in Bowling Green, Kentucky for the past 30 years. Candace and her husband, Brian, have five grown children and four grandchildren, to date. Along with their country poodle pup, Willadeen, and her sidekick, Gracie, Candace and Brian love living in beautiful rural Warren County, between Woodburn and Rich Pond. Candace has worn several hats throughout her life, both figuratively and literally, but has discovered being a grandmother to be her most beloved role. For the last decade, Candace has been blessed to be a "Granny Nanny" for her four darling GranAngels. Each of them are her inspiration to write this book and desire to share treasured messages for both young and old. *Willadeen The Rainbow Queen* follows her first book, *GranAngel Love*, released in 2020.

Award winning author-illustrator Elizabeth Rose Hoffman lives in a vintage camper nestled in Honeysuckle Holler on her family's farm in Glasgow, Kentucky. Located nearby is her studio where she writes, designs and illustrates full time. She has written and illustrated a stack of picture books including: *Here I'm Happy*, *A Goat with Many Coats*, and *Paddy the Pack Rat Pirate*. Many of her books are inspired by farm life and the many unforgettable adventures with her beloved dancing goats, sassy chickens and pouncing puppies. She feels incredibly blessed by God to do what makes her heart glad while bringing delight to those around her through her art and stories.

CPSIA information can be obtained
at www.ICGtesting.com
Printed in the USA
LVHW070552111122
732864LV00009B/142

9781088038451